Maple Syrup Season

by ANN PURMELL

illustrated by
JILL WEBER

Holiday House / New York

Uncle John leads the horse. It pulls the sled that carries Hannah and Hayden through deep snow. They are breaking out a trail from the farmhouse to Grandpa's sugar bush. Sap is running in the old sugar maple trees.

It is the time the Brockwell family comes together to make maple syrup.

SAP'S RISING!

Grandpa drills a hole and hammers in the spout. He hangs a bucket. Soon the first *plunk* of sap hits the metal bottom.

"Sap's rising!" Grandpa shouts. The family cheers and claps mittened hands.

Grandpa,
the uncles,
and Dad
drill holes.

Two bigger cousins follow and
clean out the holes with twigs.

Grandma, Aunt Haddie, and Mom hammer in spouts.

Hannah and Hayden hang buckets while three younger cousins put hats on them.

The sun fades as the last bucket and hat are hung. If there is warm sunshine, the buckets will fill with sap in a day or two. If the wind blows freezing air and the sky is thick with clouds, it will take longer.

"I'll keep an eye on the buckets," Grandpa says. "Grandma will telephone when it's time to take the sap to the sugarhouse."

Three days later the buckets brim with clear sap and the family is back in Grandpa's sugar bush. Mom and Aunt Haddie prepare the sugarhouse.

Dad helps the uncles
pour sap from the tree
buckets into gathering
buckets and then
into a giant barrel
on the sled.

Uncle John leads the horse to the sugarhouse. It takes all of the grown-ups together to tip the barrel.

A stream of sap flows down the gutter to the storage tank. From the storage tank, sap now pours into the evaporating pans. Flames shoot from the firebox and lick the bottoms of the pans.

The sap bubbles and pops as it boils. Boiling sap must be carefully watched. Not enough heat and it will not turn to syrup. Too much heat and the sap burns or even explodes.

Uncle Fred's job is to feed the fire. Grandpa tests the temperature. Dad and Uncle John take turns skimming the sap to remove dirt and bark.

A maple fog fills the sugarhouse and rolls out the windows and door.

Hannah's and Hayden's cheeks are mapley wet.

The temperature in the finishing pan creeps to 218°F. Grandpa whoops, "It's sheeting!"

The children cheer, "Hooray!" The sap is now syrup.

Uncle John opens the spigot and a golden stream cascades into a bucket.

He closes the spigot and Grandpa sees if the hydrometer floats. If it does, the syrup is poured through a flannel-lined funnel into a filtering tank.

Grandpa pours syrup into
small sample jars to grade it.

This first batch of syrup is pale gold or Fancy Grade. The syrup that comes next is darker; it's called Grade A. The last syrup of the season will be darkest and sweetest. It's called Grade B.

Tonight a maple moon will rise when Grandma tucks in Hannah and Hayden alongside the cousins. Meanwhile, the grown-ups work in the sugarhouse, making syrup until sunrise.

The sun tops the trees and snowflake wisps float on air.

After breakfast Hannah and Hayden smooth down
a mound of freshly fallen snow with brand~new rakes.
Grandma dribbles warm syrup, which quickly turns from
sparkling rivers and ponds into sweet, chewy taffy.

SUGAR ON SNOW!

Grandma calls only once, "Sugar on snow!"
The family comes running. They drop to
their knees and pick up the taffy. Grandma
has forks for Mom and Aunt Haddie, who
like to twirl the candy before eating it.
Even Grandpa and Grandma kneel beside
Hannah and Hayden.

The whole Brockwell family grins and
laughs. They know that the sugary treat
means spring will be coming soon.

Maple Syrup Lore

Native Americans were the first to make maple syrup. They used the syrup to season corn, meat, and fish. During the month some called Maple Moon or Sugar Moon, tribes held festivals to celebrate spring and maple syrup season. Native Americans taught European settlers how to make maple syrup.

There are many legends of how maple syrup was discovered. One story tells how a Native American threw his hatchet into a maple tree on a cold winter night. The next morning he pulled out his hatchet and went hunting. A bowl happened to be sitting under the tree gash; and as the day grew warmer, sap slowly dripped, but no one noticed. At dinnertime the man's wife became distracted and did not realize her meat had boiled dry and was about to burn. When she saw dinner was going to be ruined, she emptied the bowl of thin, clear liquid that looked like water into her pot. It saved her meat and made a sweet, maple-flavored sauce.

Maple syrup is graded by the standards of the USDA (United States Department of Agriculture) based on color:

Fancy Grade or **Grade A-Light Amber** is the palest of all syrups. It has

a delicate, sweet flavor with a hint of maple and is about the color of apple juice.

Grade A-Medium Amber is a darker shade with a color similar to apple cider vinegar. It has a stronger mapley-sweet flavor than Fancy.

Grade A-Dark Amber is the darkest. It looks approximately the same color as apple cider. It is the sweetest syrup with the strongest maple flavor.

Grade B is thick, dark, and heavy. It is syrup with a highly concentrated, sweet maple flavor and is used in baking or to make products such as barbecue sauce.

Vermont produces more maple syrup than any other state. New York, Maine, New Hampshire, Massachusetts, and Connecticut also produce substantial amounts. Other maple syrup–producing states range from Utah to Michigan, Ohio, and Virginia. Quebec, Canada, also produces maple syrup.

Several types of maple trees produce sap for syrup, including the red maple, black maple, and silver maple; but more maple syrup comes from the sugar maple than from any other type.

A maple tree must be at least forty years old before it is large enough to have its sap tapped without the tree being harmed.

Maple syrup season usually lasts four to six weeks, starting in early February and ending in late April. The season varies from place to place. Once the maple trees begin to bud, the syrup becomes bitter and syrup season is over.

It takes 4–5 taps to yield about 40 gallons of sap, which boil down to 1 gallon of syrup.

Sap can only be tapped when it is moving through the tree trunk. On warm days (of 40° to 50°F) sap rises, and then on cold nights (mid to upper 20s°F) it settles back toward the roots. Some of the moving sap drips through the spout into a bucket.

The equipment in a sugarhouse is cleaned and sterilized before making maple syrup.

Maple Syrup Glossary

Breaking out: making a trail through snow from the sugar bush to the sugarhouse to transport the heavy gathering tank. This trail may be made by a horse-drawn sled or wagon or even a snowmobile.

Bucket hat: a cover for the bucket that prevents things from falling into the sap.

Evaporator: an apparatus for removing water from maple sap. Sap is poured into the evaporator's long shallow pans, and the fire underneath heats the sap until it boils. When enough water is boiled off and the liquid thickens, it's maple syrup.

Filtering tank: a receptacle that removes debris from the syrup as it flows through the tank's filter(s). The filters are lined with felt, cotton, and/or paper to collect impurities. Filtering makes syrup crystal clear.

Finishing pan: the last evaporator pan, where sap becomes thick enough to be maple syrup.

Firebox: contains the fire needed to boil sap into syrup. The firebox is located under the evaporator pans. Although the fire may be made with coal, gas, oil, or electricity, it is usually a wood fire.

Gathering buckets: sap from tree buckets is dumped into these larger buckets, then poured into the gathering tank that is then taken to the sugarhouse.

Gathering tank: a large barrel that holds sap from the gathering buckets. It is very heavy and is hauled to the sugarhouse on a sled, wagon, or pickup truck, or by tractor.

Hydrometer: an instrument that floats in the maple syrup and measures its density. If the liquid is too thin it will ferment and taste sour. If it is too thick it will form sugar crystals in the storage container.

Running of sap: the movement of sap in the trunk of a maple tree.

Sap: thin, sweet liquid a tree makes to provide energy so it can grow. Only a very small amount of the sap a tree needs is tapped, so its growth is not harmed.

Sheeting: the moment when sap becomes syrup. The syrup falls slowly from a spatula or ladle in a sheetlike stream and not in the quick, small, individual drops when it is thin.

Spout: short nozzle tapped by a hammer into the hole in a maple tree through which sap drips into a bucket. Also called a spile.

Storage tank: a receptacle that holds sap until it's time to begin the boiling process. Sap flows from the storage tank to the evaporator.

Sugar bush: an area where maple trees grow.

Sugar on snow: chewy, taffylike candy produced when warm maple syrup is poured on fresh, clean snow. It can be twirled with a fork like spaghetti or picked up with fingers.

Sugarhouse: a building near the sugar bush that holds the equipment needed to boil sap into maple syrup.

To Robbie Curtis
A. P.

In memory of Butch, our orange cat
J. W.

Text copyright © 2008 by Ann Purmell
Illustrations copyright © 2008 by Jill Weber
All Rights Reserved
Printed and Bound in Malaysia
The text typeface is Steam.
The artwork was created with gouache, Caran D'Ache, gesso,
and Saran Wrap, to create texture, on Strathmore 500 series paper.
www.holidayhouse.com
First Edition
1 3 5 7 9 10 8 6 4 2

Library of Congress Cataloging-in-Publication Data
Purmell, Ann.
Maple syrup season / by Ann Purmell ; illustrated by Jill Weber. — 1st ed.
p. cm.
Summary: Grandpa leads the way as his family works
together to tap maple trees, collect sap, and make syrup.
ISBN-13: 978-0-8234-1891-6 (hardcover)
ISBN-10: 0-8234-1891-X (hardcover)
[1. Maple syrup—Fiction. 2. Family life—Fiction.]
I. Weber, Jill, ill. II. Title.
PZ7.P977Map 2008
[E]—dc22
2006003455